Tony Bradman has written many books for children of all ages, and has been published all over the world. He has also edited a large number of highly successful anthologies of short stories and poems, including *Give me Shelter* and *Under the Weather* for Frances Lincoln. His other books for Frances Lincoln are *This Little Baby, Look Out He's Behind You* and *Has Anyone Seen Jack?* Tony lives in Beckenham, Kent.

Eileen Browne worked as a school teacher and youth worker before becoming an author and illustrator. Her best known books are *Handa's Surprise, Handa's Hen* and *No Problem*. *Handa's Surprise* and *No Problem* were both shortlisted for awards. Eileen lives in Wiltshire.

Tony and Eileen have also worked together on *Through my Window* and *In a Minute*, both published by Frances Lincoln.

For Irma the Squirmer and Mum – E.B.

For Janetta – T.B.

Text copyright © Tony Bradman 1988
Illustrations copyright © Eileen Browne 1988

First published in Great Britain in 1988 by Methuen Children's Books Ltd

This edition published in 2011 by Frances Lincoln Children's Books,
4 Torriano Mews, Torriano Avenue, London NW5 2RZ
www.franceslincoln.com

A catalogue record for this book is available from the British Library.

ISBN 978-1-84780-181-4

Printed in Heshan, Guangdong, China by Leo Paper Products Ltd in October 2010

1 3 5 7 9 8 6 4 2

WAIT AND SEE

Tony Bradman and Eileen Browne

F

FRANCES LINCOLN
CHILDREN'S BOOKS

It was Saturday,
and Jo wanted to go out.

"I've saved up all my money,"
she said to her mum.
"Can we go shopping?
I'd like to buy something."

"OK, Jo," said Mum.
"I've got to post this parcel
to Granny, anyway."

It was Granny's birthday next week.
Jo had made her a special birthday card.

"We can post your card, too," said Mum.

Jo's dad said that he would make lunch.

"Bye!" they said.
Jo's dad waved.

Jo patted Patch the dog on the head,
and off they went.

They had to go past the shops
on the way to the post office.
The first one they came to was the baker's.

They stopped to chat with Mrs Tomaselli.
She said Jo must have grown at least
one inch since last Saturday.

Jo looked at
the lovely cakes
in the window.
Should she buy one
with her money?

"No," thought Jo.
"I'll wait and see."

The next shop they came to
was the greengrocer's.

They stopped to chat with Mr Singh.
He said Jo must have grown at least
two inches since last Saturday.

Jo looked at
the lovely,
juicy red apples
in the window.

Should she buy one
with her money?
"No," thought Jo.
"I'll wait and see."

Next they came to the fish shop.
They stopped to chat with Mrs Brown.

She said Jo must have grown at least
three inches since last Saturday.

Jo looked at the fish,
and the lobsters
and crabs
and shells and ice
piled up in the window.

Should she buy something with her money?
But what would she want a fish for?
"No," thought Jo. "I'll wait and see."

At last, they came to the post office.
There were lots of people waiting
in a line.

They had to wait
a long time.

WE CLOSE AT
1 P.M.
ON SATURDAY

And when they got to the counter . . .
Jo's mum realised that she had left
her money at home!

She couldn't post
Granny's present,
or the card
Jo had made.

Now they wouldn't reach Granny
in time for her birthday.
There was only one thing to do.

"I've got some money,"
said Jo. "I'll pay!"

Jo's mum said that she would
give her the money back
when they got home.

She also said that Jo
was a very good girl.
Jo smiled.

On the way home,
Jo's mum told everybody she met
what a nice thing Jo had done.

Mrs Brown said Jo was good,
and gave her a present –

a great big fish!

Mr Singh said Jo was very good,
and gave her a present –

lots of
lovely, juicy
red apples!

And Mrs Tomaselli said Jo was very,
very good and gave her a present too –

some lovely cakes!

Which was just as well –

for when they got home,
Dad had some bad news.

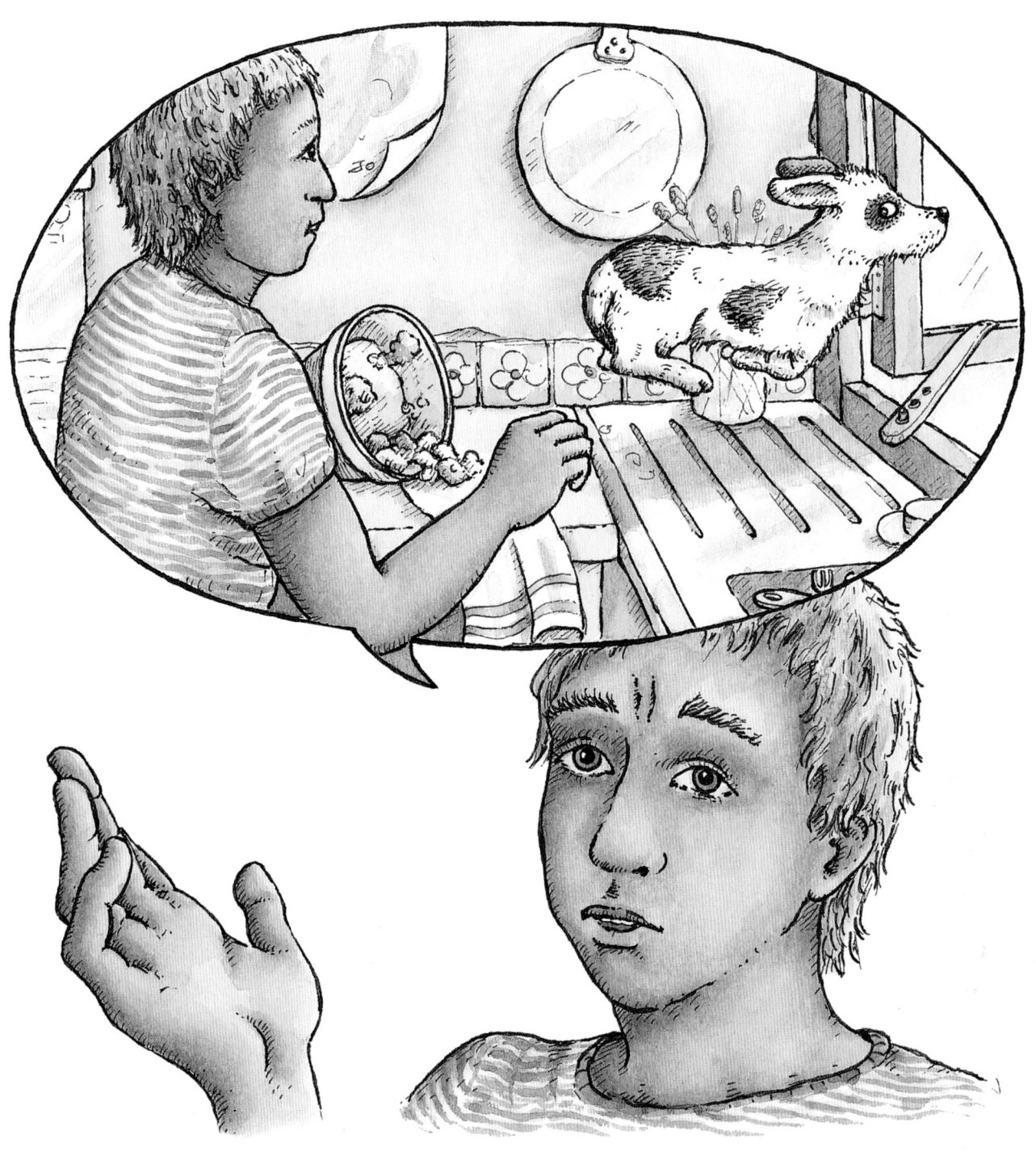

Patch the dog had eaten their lunch!
Jo's dad didn't know what to do.
"Whatever shall we have to eat?" he said.

Jo and her mum laughed.
"You'll have to wait and see!"

MORE PAPERBACKS FROM FRANCES LINCOLN CHILDREN'S BOOKS

Through My Window
Tony Bradman and Eileen Browne

When Jo has to stay in bed for the day, her dad looks after her and her mum promises to bring her a special surprise present home from work. While Jo waits, she looks out of her window at all the goings-on in the street, and gets more and more excited about what her mum's special surprise will be. . .

Billy and Belle
Sarah Garland

Billy and Belle can't wait for Mum to have the new baby! When the special day arrives, Dad takes Mum to hospital while Belle is allowed to spend the day with Billy at school. It's pet day, so Billy's hamster comes too. Everything goes according to plan – until Belle gets into a spot of trouble over a pet spider!

Lucy's Rabbit
A Lucy and Alice story
Jennifer Northway

Lucy is busy making decorations for her mum's birthday with the help of her cousin Alice. When they discover a rabbit eating Dad's pansies they think it is a great idea for a surprise present. But keeping the rabbit out of trouble for long enough to give her to Mum is harder than they expect.

Frances Lincoln titles are available from all good bookshops.
You can also buy books and find out more about your favourite titles,
authors and illustrators on our website: www.franceslincoln.com